Usborne Big Activity Book DINOSAURS

Illustrated by Christine Sheldon

Designed by Sharon Cooper

Words by Kirsteen Robson

Edited by Rosie Dickins

Dinosaur names can be tricky to say. Look out for labels telling you how to say them, or scan this QR code to hear a recording. (Or visit **usborne.com/Quicklinks** and type in the name of this book.)

Shadowy shape

Which dinosaur matches the shadow? Find and draw around it.
The long crest on its head may have helped it make honking sounds.

Feathery twins

Velociraptors were turkey-sized dinosaurs covered in feathers. Draw a line from each Velociraptor to one that looks just like it.

Dangerous diver

All kinds of swimming reptiles lived at the same time as dinosaurs. Many had large jaws full of sharp teeth for hunting. Fill in the huge underwater hunter below.

Rhomaleosaurus
("ro-MAL-ee-uh-SORE-us")

Changing seas

Some creatures from dinosaur times, such as starfish, still exist today. Others died out long ago. Circle a starfish. Then spot three differences between the pictures.

Ancient animals

Stegosaurus was a dinosaur that roamed the Earth over 150 million years ago. Use stickers to show some of the other creatures that lived at the same time.

Stegosaurus
("STEG-uh-SORE-us")

In the swamp

While dinosaurs roamed the land, some other animals lived in swamps.
Join the dots in order, to show what one of them looked like.

Fishy diet

Some dinosaurs used their hook-like claws to catch fish.

Draw around the squares that match the ones in the picture above.

Different stripes

Which dinosaur has the most stripes on its body? Draw around it.

Can you find the dinosaur with the fewest stripes on its head crest? Draw around its head.

Corythosaurus
("kuh-RITH-uh-SORE-us")

Search by starlight

Can you spot all the things shown in circles below in the scene?

Tremendous Triceratops

Triceratops was a dinosaur as big as an elephant, with horns as long as golf clubs. Fill in this Triceratops.

How to draw a Triceratops

1 Draw a body and head like this.

2 Add curved lines for a tail, and rectangles for its legs.

3 Draw two curved horns on the head and one on the nose.

4 Draw half circles on the back and add a face.

Draw more Triceratops in the space above.

Mystery egg owner

Dinosaurs laid eggs with their baby dinosaurs inside. But which dinosaur laid THESE eggs? Follow the clues below to find out, then circle it.

It is purple...

Maiasaura
("MY-uh-SORE-a")

Therizinosaurus
("THER-i-ZIN-uh-SORE-us")

It has spikes...

Australovenator
("OST-ruh-luh-VEN-uh-tor")

Stegosaurus

...and it is eating leaves.

Ankylosaurus
("an-KIE-luh-SORE-us")

Parasaurolophus

Family features

Dinosaurs were born with features such as frills and horns, which got bigger as they grew. Looking at their features, can you match each big dinosaur to its baby?

Underwater animals

Here are some types of sea creatures that lived during dinosaur times.
Circle the picture in each row that doesn't match the others.

Fish

Ammonite ("AM-uh-nite")

Archelon ("ARK-uh-lon")

Jellyfish

How to draw a jellyfish

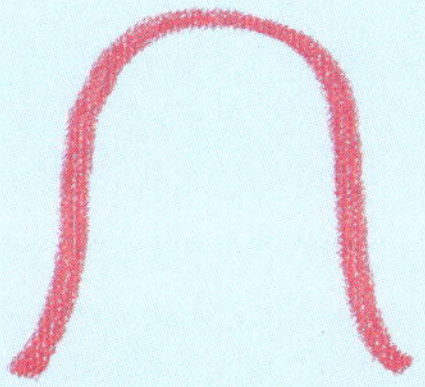

1 Draw a bell shape.

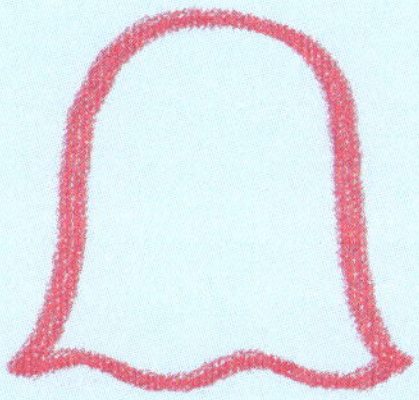

2 Add a wavy line across the bottom.

3 Add wiggly lines for tentacles.

4 Then draw on a face.

Add more jellyfish floating in the sea.

Hungry hunters

These dinosaurs hunted other animals for food. One of them doesn't match the rest. Find and draw around it.

Safe landing?

These tiny feathery dinosaurs weighed no more than a bag of sugar. Which one will land on the branch? Follow the trails to find out, then draw around the dinosaur.

Summer days

By 75 million years ago, many kinds of animals lived alongside dinosaurs. Add stickers to arrange insects, snakes and furry mammals with the dinosaurs in this scene.

Young Pachycephalosaurus
("PACK-ee-SEFA-luh-SORE-us")
Triceratops

Impressive crests

These flying reptiles had big head crests – probably to help them look impressive to each other. Spot three differences between the two scenes.

Pteranodon ("ter-AN-uh-don")

Spiky leaf-lovers

Ankylosauruses were covered in spikes that protected them from enemies. They ate low-growing plants. Follow the trails to see where they have been. Which one nibbled a leaf?

Desert-dwellers

Some dinosaurs lived in hot, dry deserts. Who is standing on the sand below? Find out by joining the dots in order.

Staying together

Some dinosaurs lived in groups called herds. Can you find and circle four differences between these groups?

Swooping and soaring

This flying reptile used its wide wings to swoop and soar, and its long beak to catch fish. Fill in the big one below.

How to draw a Gnathosaurus

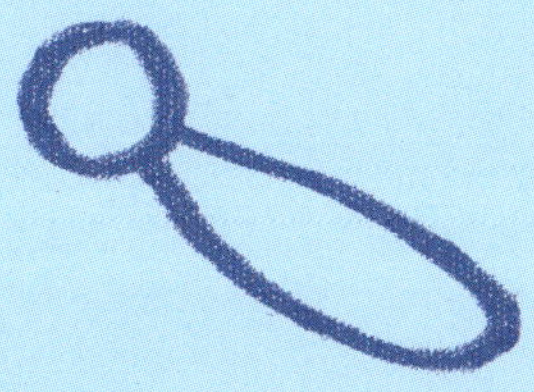

1 Draw a long body, and a circle for the head.

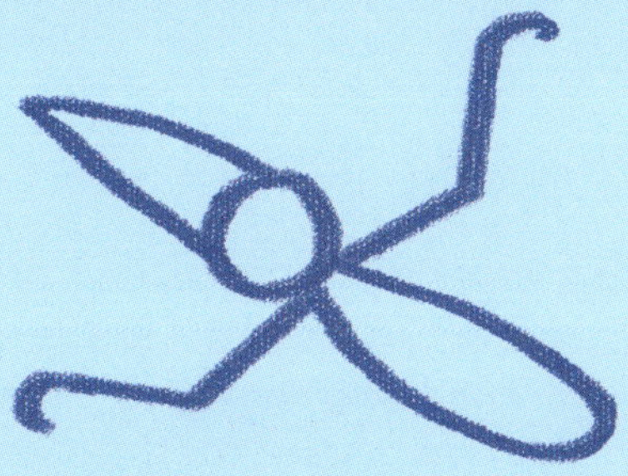

2 Add a triangle for the beak and lines for arms.

3 Draw two feet, and a wing under each arm.

4 Add a face, and a line on the beak.

Fill the sky with more Gnathosauruses.

Going fishing

Spinosaurus was the biggest of the hunting dinosaurs – with a spiny back that made it look even bigger. Can you help it find its way to the river to go fishing?

Mixed menu

This dinosaur ate plants, insects, small animals and maybe even eggs. Can you help it find the nest with the most eggs? And five tasty butterflies? Circle them.

Buried fossils

Fossils are the hardened remains or traces of animals and plants that died long ago. Draw around the fossil in each row that is the odd one out.

By the river

Rivers were home to huge reptiles – some longer than a bus – as well as lots of smaller animals. Find and circle the following small animals in the picture.

1 dragonfly

2 orange fish

3 frogs

Plates and spikes

Stegosauruses had bony plates along their backs and sharp spikes on their tails. Draw over the dotted lines to finish the two below.

How to draw a Stegosaurus

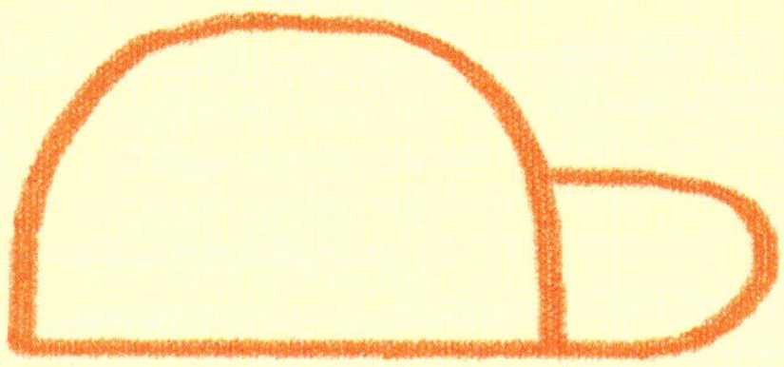

1 Draw a body and head like this.

2 Add curved lines for a tail, and rectangles for its legs.

3 Draw four triangles on the back.

4 Add four tail spikes and a face.

Use the space above to draw your own Stegosauruses.

Above the waves

Some flying reptiles ate fish, grabbing them from the water with long beaks. Use stickers to show more reptiles in the air and fish in the sea.

Happy families

Which way should the baby Styracosaurus go to find its mother? They have the same markings on their backs.

Diplodocus differences

Diplodocus was a huge dinosaur. It used its long neck to reach leaves on low bushes and high trees. Can you spot five differences between these Diplodocus scenes?

Diplodocus ("dip-luh-DOKE-kus")

Dangerous tail

A Stegosaurus could see off enemies with one swish of its strong, spiky tail. Fill in this Stegosaurus.

Shadow match

Stegosauruses probably used their back plates to help recognize each other.

Which Stegosaurus matches this shadow? Circle it.

Stegosaurus

Big-eyed sea monsters

The blue eyes below could grow as big as dinner plates – but who do they belong to? Join the two sets of numbered dots to find out.

Temnodontosaurus
("TEM-nuh-DON-tuh-SORE-us")

Mystery prints

Each kind of dinosaur left different-shaped footprints. Follow the lines to match these dinosaurs to their prints.

Insect-eaters

These dinosaurs used their strong claws to break open dead trees, to feed on the insects inside.

Can you find all the things listed below and circle them in the scene?

Terrible teeth

Did you know Tyrannosaurus rex's longest tooth was as big as an ice-cream cone? Fill its mouth with big, sharp teeth in the picture below.

Tyrannosaurus rex
("tie-RAN-uh-SORE-us-REX")

Large leaf-eater

Fill in this huge beast. It grew as long as two buses and munched leaves from the tallest trees.

Giant of the skies

Meet the biggest flying reptile ever. It was as tall as a giraffe, with wings as wide as a small plane. Can you spot five differences between these pictures of it?

Hatzegopteryx ("HATZ-uh-GOP-ter-ix")

Eggs and babies

All dinosaurs laid eggs – some a few at a time, others up to 40. Use stickers to fill these pages with more dinosaurs, eggs and babies.

Maiasaura

Stenonychosaurus
("STEN-uh-NIE-kuh-SORE-us")

Under the sea

Archelon was a giant sea turtle, with a shell the size of a small car. Ammonites were smaller sea creatures with spiral shells. Can you spot three ammonites? Then look for the other creatures listed below, and circle them in the scene.

How to draw an Archelon

1 Draw a shell and head like this.

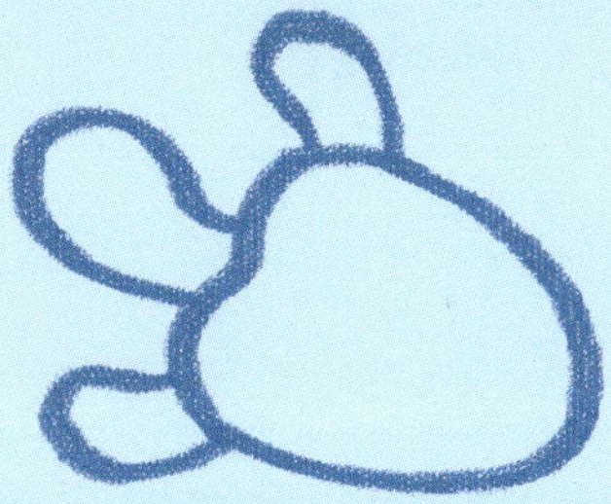

2 Add two curved front flippers.

3 Then draw two back flippers.

4 Add a face and tail, and spots on the shell.

Draw more Archelons in the sea.

Leafy lunch

Can you help this dinosaur find the shortest path to its baby? How many plants can it eat along the way?

Answer: ....

Triple-horned Triceratops

Triceratops means "three-horned face". Spot five differences between these two Triceratops pictures.

Racing dinosaurs

Many dinosaurs walked or ran on two legs. All these dinosaurs are running in the same direction, except one. Can you find it?

Searching for food

Some of the things dinosaurs ate are listed below.
Can you find them hidden in the grid?

i	r	s	s	m	i	l	o	s
e	s	t	n	a	o	s	f	i
l	s	s	u	g	n	s	i	n
t	d	e	h	r	d	o	s	s
e	e	s	e	r	t	g	h	e
l	n	f	a	h	g	l	a	c
s	d	z	i	e	t	n	e	t
d	i	n	o	s	a	u	r	s
l	e	a	v	e	s	n	a	m

~~ferns~~ leaves

moss dinosaurs insects

eggs turtles fish

lizards

Frosty forests

Some dinosaurs had to cope with dark, snowy winters. They often had fuzz or feathers to keep them warm. Draw over the dotted lines and fill in the stripes to finish this fuzzy dinosaur.

Find a friend

Can you show the baby dinosaur at the bottom of the page the way to its friend among the trees?

Claws, teeth and jaws

Different dinosaurs could defend themselves – or attack other animals – using the body parts listed below.

Can you fit all these words into the grid?

horns

teeth

claws

neck frill

spikes

jaws

Butting heads

These dinosaurs had an extra thick, bony skull – perfect for butting their rivals. One of the bone-headed dinosaurs below is different from the rest. It's missing something – can you draw it in?

Fine feathers

The bird-like dinosaurs below were about the size of magpies. There are five differences between the pictures. See if you can spot them all.

Archaeopteryx ("ARK-ee-OP-ter-ix")

Compsognathus
("COMP-so-NAYTH-us")

A head full of horns

This chunky dinosaur was bigger than a rhino. It was armed with horns on its nose, cheeks and neck frill. Fill it in.

In the moonlight

Not all dinosaurs slept at night. Add stickers to show who might have been out and about in the moonlight.

Diplodocus

Answers

2

3

5

8
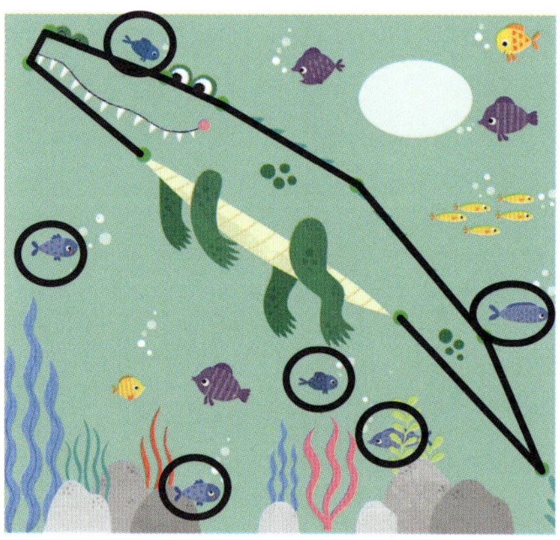

9

10

11

14

15

16
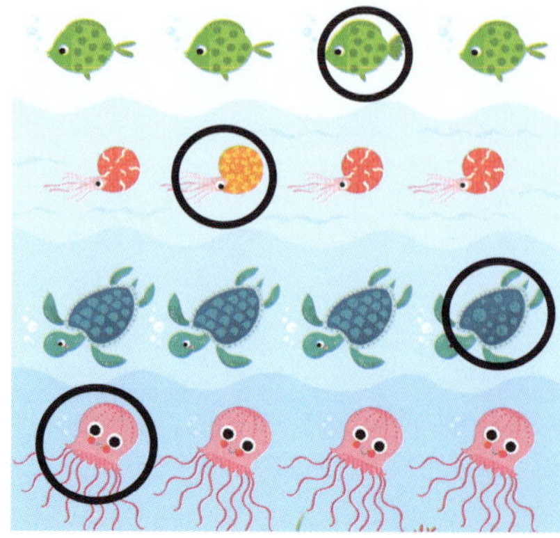

18

19

22

23

24

25

28

29

30

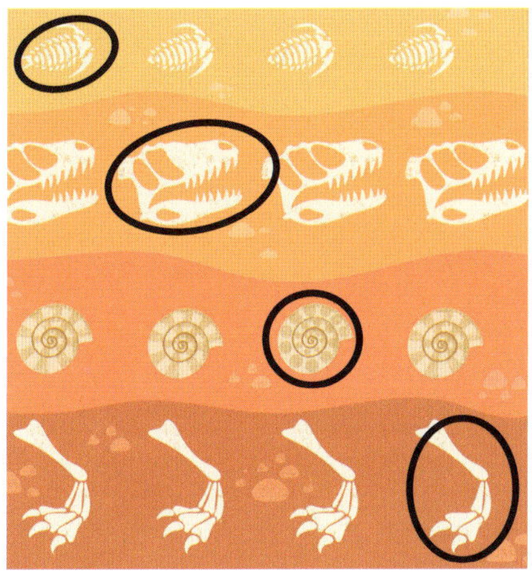

31

36

37

39

40

Answers

41

42

45

48

50

51

52

53

55

56

57

58